# FUNNYMAN'S FIRST CASE

# FUNNYMAN'S FIRST CASE

**An Easy-Read Story Book**

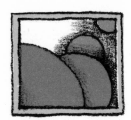

by Stephen Mooser
illustrated by Tomie de Paola

**Franklin Watts**
New York/London/Toronto/Sydney
1981

E
MOO

**FOR BRYN,**
**my own little funny man**

**R.L. 2.2 Spache Revised Formula**

Library of Congress Cataloging in Publication Data

Mooser, Stephen.
  Funnyman's first case.

  (A Easy-read story book)
  SUMMARY: A wisecracking waiter uses some of his
best jokes to foil a robbery.
  [1. Jokes—Fiction.   2. Crime and criminals—Fiction]
I. De Paola, Thomas Anthony.   II. Title.
PZ7.M78817Fu              [E]              80-29637
ISBN 0-531-03538-7
ISBN 0-531-04300-2 (lib. bdg.)

Archie was a waiter at King's Cafe.
He loved making people laugh. So,
along with the food, he served jokes.

One morning a man said, "Waiter,
this coffee tastes like mud!"
"Of course it does," said Archie. "It
was ground this morning!"

Another time somebody asked, "Do you serve crabs here?"
"Sure, we serve anyone. Sit right down," laughed Archie.

Luckily, Mr. King didn't always hear
Archie joking about the food. That's
because he was usually busy watching
his money.
He was afraid of being robbed by
the famous crook, Big Red.

"Big Red has robbed every shop in town," said Mr. King. "Yesterday he stole two rare coins from the Ace Coin Shop."
Archie held up a coin and smiled.
"Maybe Big Red has been sick, and he decided the change would do him good."

Mr. King rolled his eyes. "Listen, Archie, there's nothing funny about Big Red — or about my food either. If you don't stop telling those silly jokes, I'll have to get rid of you."

Later that day a woman asked, "Is there stew on the menu?"
"There was," Archie said, "but I wiped it off!"

"Archie," said Mr. King crossly, "I told you not to tell any more jokes about the food. I'm giving you just one more chance. Here comes my best customer, Mr. Plum. He hates jokes. So please, none of your wisecracks."

Archie tried to be a good waiter.
He brought Mr. Plum a bowl of soup.
"I hope you like it, sir," he said.

"What's this floating in the soup?"
asked Mr. Plum.
"I don't know," said Archie. "All bugs
look alike to me."

Mr. Plum's face turned red. "I'll tell
you what it is. It's a fly!"
"Don't worry about it," said Archie.
"The spider on the bread will take
care of it."

Mr. Plum got to his feet.
"This soup isn't fit for a pig!"
"I'll take it right back and bring you
some that is," laughed Archie.

Mr. Plum stomped out of the cafe.
Mr. King was very mad. He ran over
to Archie and said, "That's it. I'm
going to get another waiter!"
"Thanks," said Archie. "I could use
the help."

Mr. King exploded. "You're fired.
Out! Out!"

Suddenly Archie saw someone taking
money from the cash box.
"Jumping Jokers!" he said to himself.
"It's Big Red."

Archie didn't know what to do. No
one was near Big Red. If he yelled,
the crook would get away.
Then he thought of a plan. "I'll
knock him out with a joke."

"Who knows why the crook took a
  bath?" said Archie.
When Big Red heard the word
  "crook" he looked up.
"He took a bath so that he could
  make a clean getaway." Big Red
  smiled.

Now that he had the robber's attention, he began hurling jokes like lightning bolts.
"I parked my car and got a ticket. I don't know why I got the ticket. The sign said FINE FOR PARKING."

"You know what animal eats the least?
A moth. All he eats are holes."

Mr. King couldn't work out what was going on, but he didn't stop Archie. He was enjoying the jokes. And so was Big Red.

"I keep seeing spots before my eyes," said Archie.

"Have you seen a doctor?" asked Mr. King.

"No, just spots," laughed Archie. Big Red grabbed his sides and howled with laughter.

"This will finish him off," thought
Archie.
"This morning someone asked me if
I took a shower. I said 'no, is one
missing?' "
That did it. Big Red laughed so hard
he began rolling on the floor.

"Quick!" yelled Archie. "Get Big Red!"
In a wink the robber had been
captured. When they got Big Red to
his feet, he was still chuckling at
Archie's jokes.

"Easy, easy," he said. "I'm a little sore from laughing."

"I don't care who you are or where you're from," said Archie. "You're going to jail."

"All is forgiven," said Mr. King. "From now on I'm calling you Funnyman — the man who stops crime with jokes."

'I like that," smiled Archie. "Crime is no laughing matter, but when I'm on the job, catching the crook will be."

## About the Author and Illustrator

### STEPHEN MOOSER
is the author of many distinguished books for children, including *The Ghost with Halloween Hiccups,* on which he and Tomie de Paola first collaborated. Mr. Mooser is President of the Society of Children's Book Writers, and lives in California with his wife and two children.

### TOMIE DE PAOLA
has illustrated over one hundred children's books. More recently, he has written text as well for a number of notable books. A recipient of numerous prizes and awards, Mr. De Paola lives in a one-hundred-fifty-year-old farmhouse in New Hampshire.